Expanding Consciousness

How far would you go?

Shanna Faye

EXPANDING CONSCIOUSNESS

This book is written to provide information and motivation to readers. Its purpose is not to render any type of psychological, legal, or professional advice of any kind. The content is the sole opinion and expression of the author, and not necessarily that of the publisher.

Printed in the United States of America.

ISBN   978-1-64552-045-0   (Paperback)
ISBN   978-1-64552-046-7   (Digital)

Lettra Press books may be ordered through booksellers or by contacting:

Lettra Press LLC
18229 E 52nd Ave.
Denver City, CO 80249
1 303 586 1431 | info@lettrapress.com
www.lettrapress.com

Prologue

Peru, March 8, 2019

Floor.

Floor feels really good right now…

As I'm coming to, that's where I notice I am.

On the floor in front of the toilet of the tambo allocated to me at the retreat center in the middle of the Peruvian jungle.

The second time passing out.

It feels like I cannot move.

And I know I need help.

Now!

It comes to me that I'd called out the name of the assistant manager before I lost consciousness and fell.

I'm trying 'Help!' now, and also 'Ayuda!' (which is Spanish for 'Help'.)

Finally, one of the indigenous workers hears me and appears at my entrance door. I manage to tell him in Spanish to look for the assistant manager and ask him to come as quickly as possible.

I feel so weak.

I can't, and don't want to, move.

Standing up is not an option, as it makes me faint, lose consciousness and collapse right away.

I'm not going to try that a third time.

The urge to go to the bathroom has left. I must have been able to pass the diarrhea somewhere in between. At this point I'm so catatonic, I don't care.

I just want it to stop.

The images I'm seeing now, even with my eyes open, aren't unpleasant. Whatever is going on is just too much for my nervous system and my circulation.

Why do I have to experience this?

Because I handed my power over...

Chapter 1

In my life I've never been into drugs and have never tried any.
Not even weed.
And I never smoked.
Yes, when I was 16, 17, 18 years old, I was in Paris a lot and it was kind of 'chic' or cool to be holding a cigarette and pretending. I didn't inhale the smoke and I hated the smell and taste of it.

As I started embarking on my personal healing path, exploring various healing modalities, it turned out that especially with homeopathic treatment, drugs are actually counteracting the healing or slowing it down significantly, to the point of making it impossible. This obviously supported my being adamantly against drug use.

There was also an aspect of fear of having a substance 'take over' and my not being in control of my mental faculties anymore. I didn't care much for that, still don't, and feel the same about the effects of alcohol abuse.

More recently, since end of 2018, I've started working with a new mentor and he gave me the perspective of using such an experience as a teacher. In the sense of seeing what I could learn from Ayahuasca, if I felt attracted to do so, remembering the feeling of the expanded consciousness state, and then recreating that state out of my own, without having to use the drug.

This mentor is coming from the point of view that if one has to keep using the drug to recreate the experience, it becomes a crutch and also can lead to addiction. He is very emphatic that he does not recommend doing Ayahuasca, and that it's not for everyone.

I very much resonated with his perspective and with my Druid connection, the use of plant teachers for visions in combination with fasting or cleansing wasn't a new idea. I also felt it might be a good idea to challenge my fear of losing control and face it instead, as a one-time experience within a safe space and with someone who knew what they were doing.

In addition to that, also at the end of 2018, in November, I'd attracted a new guide and he encouraged me to follow my passion, try radical new experiences (I'd say this one here counts) and make a daily practice of taking on new perspectives, even those that would be hard for me to comprehend.
Embracing everything without judgment.

So, I did some research and came across a blog post on Ayahuasca that was very honest and transparent about this person's experience; taking away any potential glamour and the notion that everyone would always be 'blissed out' on this drug. A reference was given and it sounded legitimate. Next thing I know, I'm signing up for a weeklong retreat in Peru.

My own evolution has been rather fast-paced of late, which the name change (I changed my first names to Shanna Faye legally end of 2018) seemed to have supported even more so. I've been feeling myself shifting faster and faster and felt ready to take on this challenge, as I still felt it to be a stretch for me and a leap at the same time.

It was exciting though. And I was really looking forward to it.

On registering, as I tuned into the shaman there, it felt to me like we had a deeper connection beyond this retreat experience, and I was curious to meet him.

Chapter 2

Peru, March 4, 2019

Today the participants gathered at the meeting point. We all signed waiver forms, where basically we acknowledged we are okay with dying. We have a small but eclectic and fascinating group of people:

Ofer, a light artist from Israel; he's had a show in Lima and can just make it through the three ceremonies before he'll have to go back home.

Adam and his girlfriend from Brooklyn, NY. They are both dancers, and she has her own dance company. Adam has been focusing more on various martial arts in the recent past.

Francesco, an architect from Italy, with a passion for graffiti painting. He's the only one with experience in the Ayahuasca department, and we very much appreciate his insights.

Sean, a graphic designer from Chicago, who is transitioning into starting his own business with the work he loves.

Sean and another man from Germany are joining our group on Tuesday for group circle (after the morning cleanse).

The setup at this particular retreat is a week, arriving on Monday at the center and leaving on Sunday. That includes preparation, three group ceremonies at night and an optional fourth one the morning after the third group ceremony. The optional one is in your tambo by yourself with one dose only.

[A tambo consists basically of a hut made of thin plaster dry sheet walls to chest height, the rest up to the roof is mosquito-netting, with the roof made of several layers of interwoven palm leaves.

Inside is a bed with mosquito net, a hammock, a small table, a little bench and a separate section with a toilet seat that is not anchored to the floor, but just loosely sits on it.

There is a crane for water to run into a bigger bucket and from that, you take a smaller plastic container with water to wash down the toilet.

This section is partitioned off of the main room by a chest height, plaster dry sheet wall – that's it.]

This 'purge' (the indigenous people call it 'purga') is rather violent in my experience. The human body treats Ayahuasca like a poison. Period.

It does not tolerate grandmother Ayahuasca without trying to rid itself of it sooner or later in the form of vomiting and diarrhea.

As the shaman explained to us, the Ayahuasca plant that is being used in the mixture we received, is made from the wine 'cielo' ('Heaven' in Spanish). Apparently, there are other Ayahuasca species, which are more harsh or stronger in effect, so we had a 'milder', gentler version. Contrary to what one might think, Ayahuasca is actually not the part that contains the DMT [Dimethyltryptamine is a chemical substance that occurs in many plants and animals and which is both a derivative and a structural analog of tryptamine. It can be consumed as a psychedelic drug and has historically been prepared by various cultures for ritual purposes], another plant of the mix has the DMT, with Ayahuasca acting as the MAOI [Monoamine oxidase inhibitors (MAOIs) are a class of drugs that inhibit the activity of one or both monoamine oxidase enzymes A and B. They are best known as powerful anti-depressants, as well as effective therapeutic agents for panic disorder and social phobia].

To optimize the action of the DMT, or better, ascertain that it not be impeded, a special diet is required. This ideally starts three days before arrival and throughout the retreat until after the last ceremony:

- No salt
- No sugar
- No oil
- No red meat
- No spices
- No alcohol
- No caffeine
- No sex

For most, the diet is a real issue. We were a small group of seven, which really worked for me. The week prior they had 23 participants. So there seems to be quite a bit of fluctuation.

On Monday we were still served food with a little bit of salt and taste. I didn't eat at the meals as I wasn't hungry.

We had a group session of introduction to the plants that were being used in the brew and were shown these plants on a tour around the center property in the jungle.

After that we received some more information about the procedure with the shaman reinforcing that Ayahuasca gives you what you *need*, not what you think you *want*.

(It was interesting for me to hear that again, as the mentor I mentioned earlier had emphasized this quite a bit: Life is about getting what we *need*, not what we *think we want*. They might coincide at times, but more often than not they don't. And it is always about what serves our and everyone's highest good.)

We were told that if something got too much, there was a way to cut the action of the medicine. Then each one of us had an individual interview with the shaman to let him know what we'd like to focus on or what our intention was for the ceremonies.

On Tuesday morning at 6am we had a first cleansing ritual, where we were to take an herbal cocktail and then drink four liters of water and more very fast until we would throw everything up.

An aspect of that was for us to get used to the idea of vomiting in each other's presence, as that is an integral part of each of the ceremonies.

As I mentioned earlier, the human body recognizes the Ayahuasca plant mixture as poison and will reject it as soon as it can. I'd say from what I saw there that 98% of the time you will vomit the herbs sooner or later, sometimes even right after drinking them.

If you don't vomit, the body rids itself of the mixture through the stool. More often than not it's both, depending also on the amount that was ingested.

It is a rather vulnerable experience and doesn't come easy to everyone. Having had every possible eating disorder that's out there, throwing up wasn't an issue for me, and although I'd have preferred to do this by myself, it was interesting for me to, for once, not do it in 'hiding'.

Francesco attended the morning 'cleanse' but in the afternoon I passed by his tambo and heard him moaning as though in extreme discomfort. He didn't answer my calling out to him. I didn't want to get too near and impose on his privacy so decided to get someone to check in on him. I was on my way to find the assistant manager when I ran into Ofer and asked him if he'd heard Francesco's agonizing sounds.

Ofer said he did, but he'd thought that maybe Francesco was doing some pre-ceremony ritual or something. Sweet, sweet Ofer.

I said it didn't sound like anything pre-ceremony to me, but severe discomfort, and I'd rather have him be interrupted in his 'ritual' than not check in on him.

So, I found the assistant manager and he promised to see what was going on.

It turned out Francesco was really miserable and had come down with a fever and various other symptoms. The nurse had an eye on him, but he was in no condition to attend the ceremony at night. He'd so been looking forward to it.

That night we were to start with our first ceremony. I had had a bit of a cough for the past days and the shaman advised me to take lemon water with ginger and garlic. I had this around 5:30 - 6pm with the ceremony starting at 7pm.

Another thing that is being brought to my attention I hadn't thought about: there is quite a bit of ritual smoking involved – for protection, cleansing and purification purposes – and I'm very sensitive to smoke.

Great! Can't wait to have smoke blown in my face, my hair, my clothes!

Chapter 3

Peru, March 5, 2019

So here we are. Each one of us has our own mat, a pillow, a blanket, some toilet paper and a square orange bucket to puke into.
Lovely.

The shaman started out with a silent invocation, blowing smoke on himself for protection and then made the rounds blessing and protecting everyone in the room, including his assistant and the nurse, who are both always in attendance.

Since it was pitch dark during the ceremony, with no light source, the assistant helped us when we needed anything or had to go to the bathroom. We were just to knock on the floor three times and he would come over.

We were then one by one invited to go over to the shaman to receive our first dose.
The measurement is called a 'cup' but what we are talking about is a very small glass, the size one would use for a liquor shot (~25ml).
One small glass is called a cup. You can also choose a half or three-quarters of a cup.

The shaman had recommended that we start out with one cup initially, as most of us were newbies and this our first Ayahuasca experience. During each ceremony, about an hour and a half into it, we were given the option to take another dose.

Knowing myself as being on the sensitive side and usually having a stronger reaction to a substance than others who had twice as much, I liked the approach of erring on the side of caution and starting with a lower amount. I went for one cup the first time.

After receiving the dose, we were to lie down, close our eyes and relax to see what we'd be shown by grandmother Ayahuasca.

The shaman chanted pretty much throughout the ceremony, starting out with an individual chant, blessing and smoke blowing for each person in the room. Then he blew out the three candles that were lit at the beginning of the ceremony and everything went pitch dark.

For me nothing happened. In my mind I'd been thinking that the effect would happen right away and the drug would be taking over.

Not at all.

I noticed a few geometric patterns and there were thoughts of a relationship I'd been grieving for the past weeks. But I didn't want to think about that and was able to just shift my focus.

About 20-30 minutes in, I still didn't see anything. I asked the assistant if that was normal, or what to expect, and he said it could sometimes take 40-50 minutes for the effects to start showing.

I felt slightly nauseous and my intestines were gurgling, but other than that I didn't feel much happening. When we were asked individually if we wanted another dose, I went for one and a half cups. I threw up pretty shortly after taking that dose, my body just rejected it right away and I wasn't sure if that could interfere with the action.

I learned later that it doesn't.

What with having had the lemon water earlier, I was wondering if this had prevented any response to the drug, as apparently lemon juice is used to interrupt the action of the medicine if it gets too intense.

The ceremony runs from 7pm to around 12am, so that most of the effect of the drug has faded by then. They calculate about four hours after taking a dose until one is 100% back to normal.

That means if you take a second dose after about 1.5-2 hours, the effects have not cleared completely by the end of the ceremony.

I noticed this when I went to bed that my system was still 'on' and my night was cut pretty short.

Most of us didn't get much sleep during the night, due to residual drug influence.

The next morning during group circle and listening to the experiences of the other members of our group, it became apparent that most of them had very little response and didn't feel much. There were a few who had seen geometric figures, patterns and colors. Everyone threw up though.

Sean had an experience of being forgiven, which was very pertinent for his current situation and personal healing process. So, he was quite happy and moved by his experience.

As some of the others were mentioning the geometric patterns, I remembered that I had experienced those also, but hadn't given it much thought. As a child until adolescence, I'd seen those quite frequently and they were natural, so to me it didn't feel like anything special.

I remember experiencing these patterns showing up as making me feel connected and soothing, like a haven for me to retreat into. Of course, I wasn't doing drugs at that time, and so I didn't think of it as anything special when they were shown to me the night before during the ceremony.

I also learned that one can be shown images or situations with persons that need resolution or similar. And I remembered the images of the person I'd been grieving and didn't want to think about in this moment. It seemed afterwards that this was shown to me for closure when I thought it was just a random thinking about this person again and I didn't want to go there in that moment.

What I found interesting though, and what I hadn't anticipated, however, the experiences the others shared confirmed: you could mentally influence the response to the drug. Meaning, if you didn't have your eyes closed it would stop (it's an inner seeing, not visions with eyes open). Also, if you didn't want to think about something or wanted to focus on something else, that was possible.

I'd been under the impression that the medicine would take over in any event and apparently that wasn't the case.
At least not at these smaller doses. I was going to find out a quite different scenario later.

There are physical effects though which are not negligible. Besides the throwing up, retching and heaving, the heart rate is accelerated throughout and it seems to have an impact on the metabolism. I felt hungry after that first ceremony, but also attributed it to the fact that I hadn't eaten much.

Chapter 4

Peru, March 6, 2019

In the morning before breakfast we had to take a different kind of herbal concoction, which was supposed to support us in this whole process. One ingredient was garlic – yummy on an empty stomach.

The nurse also took our blood pressure every day. Sean had a history with high blood pressure and he was allowed only very low dosing of Ayahuasca.

I'd been hungry at night after the ceremony and yet didn't have much of an appetite for breakfast. Lunch for me was rice and a bit of salad, since I don't eat beans or chicken. The fruit was lovely though: fresh papaya, mini bananas and watermelon.

Fruit was available throughout the day until about 4-5pm. No dinner, since you'd be throwing it up anyways. There was another one of the herbal cocktails we had before breakfast at 5pm that day.

I went for walks around the property every day whenever I got a chance. A lush and beautiful jungle sanctuary with two lakes we could bathe in. There were tiny, adorably cute monkeys, lizards, fish, colorful birds and four species of very busy ants. The vegetation is abundant and wild with a path hewn into it. You are in midst of mother nature, no question.

Being more of an introvert, it is quite natural for me on retreats to not be wanting any input per se. Having participated in quite a number of 10-day Vipassana silent retreats, I found myself just naturally going inward. What was different here though was, that usually, no input allows for processing, thoughts moving through, space opening up for creativity. I might get new ideas or insights, realizations. That wasn't the case this time. I felt 'blank' most of the time. It wasn't a bad experience or feeling, just different and unusual.

Also, I'd been wondering if Ayahuasca would increase sexual desire or something, since the No Sex seemed such an important part of the diet. I didn't feel that myself, although I would consider my libido to be on the higher side. From what I gleaned from my fellow participants, no one was even thinking about sex during this time, as most were just too tired, with a headache or weak.

My initial sense of connection with the shaman was confirmed. There was our shared love for nature and preserving it, a lot of natural affection in our exchange, hugging and him checking in on me on how I was doing and what was going on throughout the week.

We had a fruit bath scheduled for 11am today and I thought that, like the flower bath we had the night before, and each evening before the ceremonies, I'd just take a big cup of that water and pour it over my body after my shower.

But no, this was a different deal. The shaman actually did this for us and basically poured the fruit soup, which consisted of small pieces of banana, papaya, watermelon and some red fruit juice mix, over our heads and whole body, rubbing it into our skin.

A very sensuous experience with the rich smell of fruit cocktail and the feel of the soft fruit pieces on my skin, which I loved, but for the part of the fruit bits in my hair.

Oh well, it washed out relatively easy. We were invited to jump into the lake after being immersed and wash off the majority there instead of clogging up the showers.

I'd been checking in on Francesco, as he was a no-show for breakfast and didn't seem to get better. He'd been traveling around Peru for two weeks prior to the retreat and the question arose if he might have contracted Malaria. He was in no condition to participate and I felt for him. There wasn't much we could do, but it was decided to get him checked out at the hospital in the nearest city the following day, to make sure it wasn't Malaria.

The staff at the center were really caring throughout in my experience.

This night, for the second ceremony I still started out low, since I didn't know if the effects had been interrupted by the lemon water.

I was joking with Ofer next to me that after this retreat we'd all be having recurring visions of orange square buckets!

So, I took 1.5 cups for the first dose. Again, not much was happening as I was lying there, keeping my eyes closed, and waiting for something to be shown to me. Yes, there were some geometric shapes, but that was it. I decided to go higher on the second round and took two cups.

This time I could feel the drug action in my brain, as it seemed parts were going numb or something was infiltrating my right hemisphere. I was nauseous and I threw up, knowing now that this wouldn't impact the action of the drug.

There were some more variations of geometric patterns, colors and shapes, but since this was natural for me from childhood, I started to wonder what the hype was all about.

I then decided though that if this was all I'd experience, fine, so be it —this was what I was supposed to get from it and I didn't need to do it again. I made my peace with the situation and was, on the other hand, grateful that I didn't have any negative or upsetting things shown to me. Apparently, grandmother Ayahuasca didn't need me to process anything. Fine.

Chapter 5

Peru, March 7, 2019

Yay! Another herbal tonic before breakfast. I did actually have a bit of an appetite that morning, especially for fresh papaya. That was clearly my favorite.

Even lunch felt good and I didn't mind the flavorless food. I always feel it allows my system to readjust to less of everything, and I become more sensitive to and aware of the individual natural tastes of the ingredients on my plate.

This time it was quinoa and a steamed vegetable mix of green beans, carrots, mushrooms and celery. There was a different kind of beans and chicken for those who wanted it.

At 11am we had a mud bath ceremony, similar to the fruit bath. The shaman was again in charge for that one, and this time I came in my bathing suit, not in the dress I wore yesterday…

I definitely did not want any mud in my hair, but was told that that was going to be part of it. Hhmrnm…

The mud they were using is called 'Golden Ice' and we looked like golden statues once he was done with us. The shaman started out with blessing signs on the front and between the shoulders and then smeared the mud on our faces, leaving nothing out, not even the eyelids. Then on to torso, arms and legs. Again, it was a rather sensuous experience, but for the mud in my hair.

Adam called me 'Golden Girl'.

We were supposed to let it dry for about 20 minutes and then again, jump into the lake to rinse off.

The mud turned out to be much more tenacious than the fruit bath and we had to really scrub to get it off of our skin. Even then, most of us still had some yellow on our bodies here and there.

My hair was a different story. Although it felt like I had gotten rid of most of it in the lake, it just wouldn't wash out. Even washing my hair several times, I still had mud in my comb and brush and the towel I used.

Hated it!

Oh well.

That night for the ceremony I increased the dosage another cup to three cups on the first round.

I just wanted to know.

It was very challenging for me to swallow those three cups at once. It felt like I was gulping it down forever.

It turned out to be my ticket to the Light. I threw up after about 15 minutes, before the effect of the drug would start, but it started sooner than the nights before and this time there was also no distracting myself from it or focusing on something else.

The drug took over – no question.

I was shown a variety of different dimensions, e.g. one with forms of creatures that looked like a cross between octopus and worm, were piled up and moving next to each other like a wall. Colors and light were much more intense and with the interdimensional art explosions there were neon colors, sparks and a brilliance that was more, or different, from what we know on this planet. There were also shapes moving inter-dimensionally, meaning, they were unfolding beyond 3D.

The experience, and what I was shown, were pleasant overall, however, I felt it to be borderline intense, and was debating if I should cut the effect. It was on the edge, and I decided to go with it.

Then I shot to the Light and that was exactly what I'd come for. It was still very intense but bearable and I wanted it to imprint itself on my nervous system, so that new neurological pathways could be created.

It felt like my crown chakra was wide open and light was coming through and going out at the same time. An intense connection to All that Is and something I'd envisioned before for me to bring in the Light onto this planet. Now I know I can do it and what it feels like.

I noticed that I would be able to recreate this state in my meditation practice, and it felt like I was actually pretty close to it. I didn't go for a second round this time, as the riding out of that wave took longer, and I needed more rest for my system to catch up and calm down. I had said I was going to do the optional fourth ceremony the next morning and was wondering if I should do it or not.

My tambo neighbor Sean said he was going for it and the dancer couple Adam and his girlfriend, in the tambo on his other side, wanted to do the optional morning one, too.

I decided to go for 2.5 or 2.75 cups to make it just a tad less intense, but allow me to reinforce the experience for a deeper impression, more neurological pathways and easier connecting to later.

Chapter 6

Peru, March 8, 2019

There was no more herbal cocktail this morning and either one opted for breakfast or the optional extra ceremony.

Ofer and the man from Germany were leaving first thing in the morning and I didn't get a chance to say goodbye to Ofer. We'd had a lovely connection in my experience.

I did my yoga practice, as I had done on the other mornings before, too, and made sure to be back in my tambo on time. It was scheduled for 7am.

The optional version in the morning is different from the nocturnal ceremonies, as it does not take place in the ceremony room, but you stay in your tambo by yourself. The shaman comes to your place and does the smoke-blowing blessings and depending on what he senses, he'll do some chanting or prayer or other form of blessing.

I saw one of the workers bring two buckets and was wondering if that meant that Adam and his partner had opted out.

The shaman came to my tambo early, at about 6:40am. We hadn't had the group circle yet, so he wasn't aware of my experience the night before. I still was debating between 2.5 and 2.75 cups when he went through the blessing, smoke blowing on my head, side, back and my hands.

Then he prepared the cup and in my experience we both didn't speak. When he lifted the carafe to the cup, he looked at me and I heard him say: 'Quatro' (which means: 'four', as in: four cups). It wasn't a question in my experience, but a statement that I heard from him.

I was surprised that he'd suggest that and something inside of me went 'Gulp!'

I hesitated, coming back to my experience last night on three cups and my inner feeling telling me that 2.75, three maximum, would be the way to go.

Why would he say four? He had never suggested any dosing for any of the participants. (During the nightly ceremonies, when we went up to receive the brew, the assistant manager would ask us how many cups we'd like as one dose, and then he would tell the shaman.)

He didn't know what had happened for me at last night's ceremony. I was certain though that he wouldn't suggest or do anything that could cause me harm.

The thought came that he knew something I didn't and, yes, I went to the Light, but maybe there was more to be discovered beyond that. It hadn't felt like total dissolution… All of that was racing through my mind and at that moment I handed my power over.

I agreed to the four cups although my inner voice, my inner being and body were all saying no!

But, because I thought someone else would know better than I what was going on in my body and system, **I went out of integrity**

and made my inner knowing less important than someone else's opinion.

How could anyone else ever know better than I what I need, or what is good for me, in any given moment?
There is only one like me.
And only one like you.
I'm my only authority, and the same goes for you.

Even if others are well-meaning and with good intentions, they most often project from their own experience or because they are trying to alleviate suffering in a way they think is conducive, when it might not be.

(E.g. people trying to force someone to eat when they're in an acute fever. In that instance the body needs all its focus on dealing with the fever and and it is counter-indicative to defer energy to the digestive system to deal with food intake. You might have noticed that you're naturally not hungry when you have a fever or the flu. This is just one simple example.)

The interesting part here is that afterwards in the group circle that day, I learned that out of 23 participants the week prior, only five did the morning ceremony. And everyone had only one cup!
What was also interesting is that the assistant manager told me later that he is usually with the shaman on the morning ceremonies. It was a first that the shaman would just go by himself.

I also learned that in the shaman's experience, he'd heard me say 'quatro' and when he said 'quatro' he meant it as: 'Are you sure?', kind of like: 'Did I hear you right?'

He knew it was too much – and so did I, if I'm honest with myself.

So, apparently, I had to experience this, else it wouldn't have gone down this way.

I took the four cups.
With apprehension, but I held my breath to get them down, ready to throw up right away.

The shaman did some extra chanting and massaging of my head in addition to chest compressions as we do with CPR, just with me standing. He then told me to lie down, close my eyes and relax.

I had plenty of water within reach, as I found that drinking water helped with the vomiting. Also, I hadn't had any food since lunch the day before. This is not unusual for me per se, but the trip the night before and the drug action on my metabolism and system had had me wake up hungry that morning.

Contrary to the other participants, I also hadn't had any protein source really in days now, since I wasn't eating the legumes or chicken.

This time I threw up about 10 minutes after taking the dose and then again some more after another 10 minutes. The effects started much faster even than the night before, with the now familiar sensations of the drug taking over my brain, only this time they were violently intense.

It was like internal fireworks going off and very fast. There were different dimensions with intense coloring, some in heightened colors and neon, but it felt like everything was overlapping, happening simultaneously and too fast to even take in.
It was disorienting.

Now my body really wanted to get rid of this stuff as soon as possible, and I felt a strong urge to go to the bathroom.

When I felt the urge and the diarrhea coming on, my body had already begun shaking, like seizures and trembling.

Clearly my nervous system was overtaxed.

Now even with my eyes open, it didn't stop. The intensely fast-paced fireworks were still on. There was also no distracting myself in any way, shape or form.

The drug had taken over.

Period.

Getting off of the bed and to the toilet, which was just around the corner, seemed like a major task and I felt dizzy, nauseous and faint on getting up. My legs were unstable and I held onto whatever was in reach to be able to stand and hold myself up. I wanted to throw up more, but there was nothing left to throw up.

Since the toilet was just the ceramic corpus with no toilet seat, I didn't want to sit on it and tried doing my business balancing on the balls of my feet with knees bent, so that my butt was over the toilet bowl. That's the last I remember…

When I came to, I was lying between the outer wall in the corner of the tambo and the toilet seat, which I had knocked out of place with my fall.

I needed help.

This had to stop.

Now.

I called out the assistant manager's name several times as loud as I could manage, at the same time having thoughts about being concerned that I'd upset my neighbors, who I thought were on their own ceremonies at the same time as me.

Then I must have collapsed again and the next time I came to, I only felt the floor.

Floor felt really good.

It took a moment to register that I now was lying on my back in front of the toilet.

I needed help.

I'd had an inner brief debate earlier, when I was still lying on the bed, whether I should ride it out or not, knowing that it could last up to four hours.

No way.

I called out the assistant manager's name again and 'Help!' a few times. When that didn't work, I tried 'Ayuda!' (Spanish for 'Help'). I have no notion how much time passed, as time was very malleable in that moment.

Eventually, I heard one of the indigenous workers at my door (thank goodness, I'd had the intuition to not lock it from the inside after the shaman left).

The worker didn't come in, respecting my privacy, but asked in Spanish how he could help. I asked him to find the assistant manager and tell him to come as fast as he could.

Sometime later the manager appeared and was shocked to find me on the floor in that state.

What I wasn't aware of at that time, since I didn't really feel anything, but for the fireworks in my head and my system being in overdrive mode, was, that through the falls, I'd incurred abrasions and bleeding scrapes on my face, the biggest one a gash from the bridge of my nose down one side to the tip, some on my forehead and cheeks.

Later I noticed two more sore spots on each side of the back of my head.

He asked me in Spanish how he could help, and I told him I wanted the lemon.

'You want the lemon?'
'Yes, I need this to stop.'

'The lemon' is a mixture of fresh lemon juice, salt and sugar (the things you're not supposed to have in your diet as long as you are doing the ceremonies, as it interferes with the DMT action and here is used to cut the action, should a trip get too intense).

'I'll be right back with it as fast as I can. Don't worry, I'll be right back.'
He kept his promise and returned in a relatively short amount of time with a soup bowl, still stirring the mixture, which apparently had just been freshly prepared.

Just the fact that he'd finally come and I knew I wasn't alone anymore, someone was there to help, was a huge relief. The intermittent shaking and trembling had started again, and when he came back, he fed me two tablespoons of the lemon mixture and said that should do the trick.

'How many cups did you take?'
'Four.'
'Four!?!'

He then asked me if I could get up.
Nope.
Wasn't happening.

So, he grabbed me under my armpits, sat me up, then lifted me to standing, fully supporting me, as I couldn't hold myself. (Good news for him, I'm rather a light weight.)

Once standing up, I noticed that the right leg of my pants was completely soiled with diarrhea and I saw the mess around the toilet.

I felt horrible. I didn't have the strength to clean up this mess. He told me not to worry, they'd take care of it.

I did my best to peel off my pants, as I didn't want to get in bed with that. I had a shirt dress on top which was only very slightly soiled, so I kept it on.

He helped me onto the bed and tried soothing words, such as that this should be weaning off soon.
How long is 'soon'?
Was my inner dialogue. The manager sat by my side and then said he was just quickly going to get the nurse to take my blood pressure. He'd be right back, not to worry.

He came back with the nurse and an indigenous woman from the center. The nurse told the manager there was no point in taking my blood pressure, as it tends to be on the very low side to begin with. I personally felt like I didn't have any at all at the moment.

The two of them were talking and sometimes the nurse would address me directly, but I couldn't make out when he did so, as he spoke as lowly as when talking to the manager. They were both right by my bedside, the nurse fussing over my nose with some alcohol and cotton pads. Internally I was going: 'What are you doing there? I want the fireworks to stop, I don't care about my nose!'

I could feel the insecurity of the nurse, who seemed a bit overwhelmed with the situation and somewhat helpless, as other than washing out my gashes with alcohol, there wasn't much else he could do.
They were glad to see that I'd thrown up the dose I had taken that morning and since the lemon juice didn't seem to be doing much, they were calculating the time for the effect to naturally wane.

In the meantime, I just felt half dead. I actually didn't care if I would make it or not. It was some interim state, interdimensional, somewhere in between worlds where nothing really mattered.

My eyes closed, I couldn't, nor did I want to, move my body. I felt weightless, like in a cloud. Every idea of movement felt like an effort. And what would be the point, really?

There was a moment when I felt a hand pressing into the sole of my left foot, kneading, stimulating with some strength, then pulling every single one of my toes. The same on my right foot.

The thought came: 'This is the shaman. He's trying to get me back into my body.'
I briefly opened my eyes and could make him out at the end of the bed. He proceeded to also massage and pull the fingers of my right hand and then left.

It felt good to have someone there and the assistant manager held my hand for a while. Then the shaking started more pronouncedly, and I thought this was a good sign. To me, my nervous system was unwinding, unravelling. It didn't look so good for the three people with me. I was glad that they didn't try to stop it though.

At one point, the woman, very kindly and caring, had brought some coconut water, and they suggested I drink some. They lifted my head, and I tried a bit but didn't really want it.

I just wanted to lie there and not be bothered. It was around 8:30-9am by then and usually the main effect of the drug had subsided after 1.5 hours. I'd taken my dose at about 6:45-6:50am and it still felt pretty acute.

The nurse left to check on my neighbor Sean, who'd also done the optional version. It turned out later that Sean had had his earphones in and therefore didn't hear my cries for help. He felt bad about it and apologized, but I was relieved I didn't scare him or interrupt his session.

Adam and his girlfriend actually had changed their minds and not participated. They'd just had it from the last ceremony the night before and didn't feel like any more. They'd gone off to the ceremony room in the morning, that's why they didn't hear me either.

The assistant manager stayed the longest with me. After some more time had passed, I found myself able to move my body to lay on my side and just hold onto his hand. At times he went outside to smoke, but assured me he'd be right there and for me to best just sleep it off.

I heard him leaving at one point.

My system was too revved up to sleep and too weak to get up. So, I just lay there with my eyes closed and a couple of times looking at the clock to see when the effect should have completely faded. 11am would have been the normal time, but I was still prostrate. A bit more alive though.

12pm came and I was still so weak but also wanted to be done with this! By then I actually was glad and grateful to be alive and wanted to be able to get back to normal. I sat myself up to drink water, hydrate and also tried a bit more of the coconut water. This time it felt good and my body was thankful for the liquid. I drank as much as I desired.

During the last hours lying on the bed, I'd thought about why that happened, why it had to happen and how this experience was serving me. I didn't beat myself up, but could see clearly that I'd handed my power over to the shaman, the moment I thought he'd know better than me, what I could handle or what my reaction to the drug was.

I was shown various other instances in my life where I'd handed my power over to another person by making them, or their opinion, more important than me or my well-being.

And it was so clear in that moment: No more.
This was not going to happen again.

If that was what it took to get to that point, fine.
It felt like I was granted a new life now.
My life.
To live as I please, no matter what anyone else thinks, says or feels about it.

The fluids had given me a bit of strength and I was able to stand up. It also felt like a good idea to try some food to nourish my body. So, I went to the dining room.

Today fish was on the menu: Paiche – some prehistoric sweet water fish. The chef served me some with a bit of salad and fish had never tasted better. We were now allowed salt and spices again, and they eased us into it with a bit of salt on the food.

I was still too weak to feel really hungry, but my system was grateful for the protein and some solid food.

People kept asking me about what had happened to my nose. I had no idea what I looked like, since there were no mirrors.

I met the shaman as I was walking around the property, enjoying the aliveness of it all. He told me he'd been concerned and we exchanged a really long hug. I told him I'd learned a lot.

It was a bit later during group circle that the misunderstanding came out about who had said and heard what. And we both agreed that it was meant to happen that way.

There were no bad feelings, although I could tell he was a bit apprehensive about maybe being reproached, which I didn't. I took full responsibility for what happened, since, even if it was my scenario with me waiting for him to finish the preparation and then ask me and me never mentioning four cups, since that wasn't even on my radar but a much lower dose, I still had said yes to the four cups. I could have said 'No, three' or 'No, two and a half'.

That was on me, not on him.

When we'd met on the property earlier, he'd said that one finds liberation through suffering, or, the price for liberation is suffering.

He had been worried about me, and I thought maybe this experience for him also showed him that at times it might be a good idea to say something when he thinks it's too much, instead of going with the participant's choice (which it hadn't even been in my experience).

The center staff graciously helped me move to a different tambo, so that I wouldn't have to deal with the mess I'd made.

And we received news that Francesco didn't have Malaria, but had contracted a virus through a mosquito carrying Dengue fever, which is a nasty experience and explained his wretchedness and symptoms. He was going to see if he felt better and would join us for the jungle tour the next morning.

He very much wanted at least to be able to experience that. And he did arrive back at the center that afternoon. All of us were really happy to have him back and that he felt well enough to join the excursion the next day.

We had chocolate tasting after lunch, as they grow their own cacao on the property. That certainly gave me a boost, and I was able to walk around the property and with my newfound appreciation for Life. I even offered reflexology to Sean and Francesco.

Yes, I was tired, everything still seemed like it was in slow motion, but it felt really good to be alive.

Adam had shared in the group circle that he'd been scared of everything after last night's ceremony and that's why he didn't do the morning one. For his partner again, nothing much had happened, same for Sean, but then they had only had 1.5 cups, max two cups, nothing beyond that. Yet Adam was barely functioning throughout the whole day and just wanted to sleep.

Adam and his girlfriend had both been showing a healthy appetite throughout the retreat so far, but today Adam is so weak and tired, he doesn't even feel like finishing the fish, although he assures me he thinks it is delicious.

I felt that everything considering, my lifeforce energy is rather strong to have bounced back the way it did.

At night during dinner, I had a longer conversation with Francesco, as he wanted to know what happened to my nose and we shared our points of view on drugs in general and particular. Although I don't fully agree with him, I still want to give his perspective here, as I feel it to be valid and informative for others.

Francesco had done three Ayahuasca ceremonies before and he feels that Ayahuasca got him off of his marijuana addiction of over 20 years. He now is growing his own mushrooms for trips and in his experience, it stimulates his creativity as a graffiti artist.

I can see his perspective and yet for me I'd much rather be able to draw on my own natural innate powers, instead of relying on a drug to stimulate my creativity. I feel that it is about cheating us of his true expression in a way. And I don't think his creativity would be less active without drugs. He says he can see my point, too.

Chapter 7

Peru, March 9, 2019

During the night I didn't sleep, as I was reliving the morning's experience and my system was still unraveling and releasing the trauma of it all.

We had a jungle exploration planned today, which is an extra optional trip outside of the ceremony package, and consists of a speed boat ride on the Amazonas to four different islands with their respective attractions.

I was amazed at how weak I was! A flight of stairs seemed like a major workout. (To give you some perspective: I usually workout twice daily with 50-60 min of cardio each, yoga routine in the morning, and strength training twice per week.)

My senses were also heightened and I was crying quite a bit. I know that it is a good sign of release, so I just allowed it to move through as it arose.

We visited a monkey rescue center, a form of zoo where they have piranhas, alligators, anacondas, monkeys, Paiche fish, and a two-toed and a three-toed sloth. The latter is available for hugging and absolutely adorable and cute. Each time the keeper took it off of one person to give it to the next, it looked like (veeeery slowly, of course) 'Heeyyy, I want to keep snuggling here.' With its dreamy little face. And when it met the new person, it just snuggled right in, as if that was the best place in the world ever.

I wanted to meet and be with the anaconda. The biggest one is about six yards long and it had been hung over the necks of four people simultaneously, as it is too heavy for one person alone. The thing is though that it is more sensitive right now, because it is close to shedding its skin, and apparently it has had it for touch.

I could feel its distress and that it had had enough, but two of our group had to grab it again to take a photo and the anaconda was miserable, trying to avoid the touch and hissing.

I cried for it. I was already sensitized but that did me in and I stayed with it, after the others have left, to calm it down and apologize. More tears after that and just hurting for the abuse and wondering why we think we can just override an animal's need for a break, disrespecting it to that extent.

It felt good to have that moment with the anaconda.

I was still upset after getting out of its cage and Francesco said he doesn't like this place either with the monkeys being in cages, etc. He kindly held me as I was sobbing about the snake – and more general release with that.

Everything felt more intense in general, and I was connecting with and connected to all. We saw amazing trees, one species called Ceiba, 300 years old, what a beauty!

The shaman rode with me in a motorcar for one stretch and we got a moment to talk about his mission, about saving and protecting nature and finding ways to live more harmoniously with it. He's come up with a wonderful fertilizer system that is plant based and has hardly any smell to it. No animal waste is used for it, however, it's amazingly powerful.

Aside from that, he's been experimenting with hybridization of plants, so that they would yield more harvest in shorter amounts of time and would also be more easily to harvest. For example, he is growing his own cacao, and where the average cacao plant can grow up to six meters high and can only be harvested once a year quite strenuously due to the height, his hybridized version is much smaller but can be harvested six times a year!

I love his work and am brainstorming with him on how to get the word out, encouraging him to train people. Apparently, he's setting things up to do so.

We also discussed plastic recycling, as this is something dear to my heart, and I've been researching machines that are solar-powered. So, we'll see if we can work something out together.

At the monkey rescue center, I used the bathroom and saw my reflection for the first time in a mirror. O-kay…
I looked like I'd been in a barfight!
Oh well.
In a way, even that doesn't matter. I don't feel shocked or marred and just know that it will heal perfectly.

What a trip.

I've been feeling much closer to myself and it still feels like everything is moving slower. Still integrating the experience, still somewhat not embodied. Like in the clouds and I'm watching things through a veil (I'm typing this one week later on 3/16/19).

There is also a sense of not having the same past anymore. The person I was grieving before is but a faint memory at the moment and more like I'm looking at it from the perspective of someone else's life, not mine.

I've still been having diarrhea the whole week since I returned, and it feels as if the effects of the drug are still not completely out of my system. It also feels like more processing is happening and these pages are a testimony to that for me.

Chapter 8

San Francisco, March 16, 2019

So, what am I taking away from this experience?
There's so much.

A new sense of appreciation for Life, my Life, is there. A more
intense connection to Life and to every single moment.

Would I do it again?
At this point I don't think so. I went into this experience with the
intention of that being a one-time thing, and I feel I got the range of
it. Even the ceremony that opened me to the Light I don't feel I need
to experience again.

Do I regret it?
No. I experienced what I was supposed to experience and although
it was extreme, I learned the lesson about giving my power away. And
that's not going to happen again.

Plus, I did get what I came for on the third night of ceremonies
and now have a physical sense of what it feels like to fully connect to
the Light. As I mentioned before, what I love about that particular

experience is that it's shown me how close I am to that in my meditation. So, clearly, you don't need to do Ayahuasca to get there.

I still feel it is not for everyone and the rather violent effect the drug has on the body with all the side effects I listed above, it is a strain on the system, no question.

Everyone needs to find for themselves if they feel they want to put themselves through this and also what their motivation is.

There are many other, much more gentle, ways to expand your consciousness than this one.

This book's intention is to give you a perspective on the whole ceremony and what can happen, for you to check in with yourself if this is really something you want to be doing.

I wouldn't recommend it per se. And I certainly don't support repeated or regular use of any kind of drug, as it defeats its original purpose as a teacher and can deviate into a crutch or addiction.

As I said before, Francesco mentioned that he finds it helpful for his creative expression, and I can't help but wonder how much more powerful it would be if he could actually tap into his own creative power without that crutch.

Again, also in terms of reaching a certain state: what does that mean for the rest of your life? That you are mostly in a 'blah' state and the drug gives you a kick or makes life worth living?

Wouldn't it be much more exciting and in alignment to be able to live your life in that state of bliss and connection out of your own power? Without the help of a drug?

Using this experience as a teacher once, okay. But now I know what it feels like and can create this experience out of my own. Which means, I'm not dependent on the drug to do that for me and I can choose to live out of this space, knowing that my creative powers are coming from within, not from an external cause that 'checks me out'.

Another aspect of it is the experience of Life always being for me. I'm always supported. No matter what. There were people showing up for me and caring for me when I was out of it. Receiving that was a good thing for me.

Also, on Sunday 10, when traveling back, I had Sean as a travel companion and it was a lovely experience.

I actually fell once more out of the motorcar taking us to a restaurant before leaving for the airport. A metal strip that was securing the side entrance of the rickshaw part had come unfastened and stuck out, but I didn't see that and when I wanted to get out of the cart, my foot got caught in it and I just fell out of the cart onto my right side into a pool of water at the curb.

Francesco who was riding with me, could only watch in disbelief as there was nothing he could have done to prevent my fall.

Unbelievable! I couldn't break the fall or hold onto anything, just dropped like a sack of cement. Needless to say, there were more abrasions and impact on my body. Oh well.

I tried to make light of it as best as I could. Thankfully the weather was warm, so my being partially soaked didn't bother me too much.

My travel companion Sean though insisted on my cleaning the wound and accepting a band aid for my knee, and he had an eye on me from then on.

So much support.

At one point the thought came that this is not for the 'faint of heart', but I notice that I do not want to use this expression, as it seems to have an inherent invitation for the 'tough guys' that they can make it through, or something along those lines. That's not the impression I wish to convey, and it would also defeat the purpose of the whole.

'Ayahuasca ceremony' can give a bit of a romantic impression, when it's anything but. So, part of my intention here is also to paint a more real picture of what is actually comprised in these ceremonies.

The biggest takeaway of all in this experience for me was the 'Aha' on what I was doing to myself when overriding my body's feedback, my inner voice, my guides (and definitely any common sense!). How much I can potentially harm myself by thinking someone else can ever know better than I what is best for me, feels right to me, where my limits are and what it means for me to be in alignment and integrity.

As I was lying on my bed, still too weak to get up, but coherent enough again to revisit what had happened and why, I was re-playing in slow motion the interaction with the shaman in the morning, looking very closely at my reaction and inquiring into my motivation for agreeing to the four cups.

I mean, I didn't even question his suggestion! Didn't even ask as to why he thought four was a good idea. It didn't occur to me to tell him my experience on three cups and that that had been borderline for me. In retrospect I'm still floored that I didn't ask him. If I had we might have cleared up the misunderstanding right there.

And I notice, this is not how it went down, so it was what was supposed to be happening.

Did I agree because I wanted him to like me? Wanted his approval? I feel I can honestly say that that was not the case, as our connection and caring for each other was mutual and without question.

The thoughts that had come after hearing him say 'quatro' were more along the lines of:

He must be sensing something about me that I'm not aware of. He must think that I'm ready for the augmentation. He must feel that I can handle four. He might want to give me the opportunity to take it to the next level.

Bear in mind also, that part of my intention for this experience was to come from a space of open curiosity, without judgment, ready to surrender control, knowing that I was potentially walking the edge here and definitely stretching some serious comfort zones.

As to walking the edge, that already had been my experience the night prior on three cups. Twice during that trip I'd had the thought of interrupting the action of the drug because I felt it to be borderline intense. So, I knew my edge then!

It wasn't in the shaman's power to know that about me and he definitely didn't want the power of deciding for me – he never did during the ceremonies.

So, why are we doing this?
Why are we handing our power over to others and where are we doing that in our everyday life?

It's rather insidious, really, as it can show up in so many subtle ways we might often not even be aware of.

- Each time we subdue ourselves and our true expression, out of fear of rejection, being judged, not acceptable, dismissed, seen as unworthy, not good enough, not deserving.
- Each time we say 'yes' to something, we actually honestly want to say 'no' to, because we're afraid of not being the good

daughter/son/spouse/parent/relative/friend/employee/ boss/coach/…someone else might expect us to be.
- Each time we go on auto-pilot when someone requests something with the add on: 'you don't mind, do you?' – as if that meant we automatically have to acquiesce.
- Each time we keep silent in the face of something we experience as out of integrity or that gives us a feeling of 'it's not right'.
- Each time we stay small, not living our highest potential for fear of ridicule, being seen as crazy or losing loved ones' approval and support.
- Each time we make someone else responsible for our happiness. That can be a significant other, a child, a parent, the president, anyone really, who doesn't show up the way we want them to. In those moments, we take it personally. Like, they are doing this TO us, when all that's really going on is they are just being themselves.

It's never personal.

They're just showing up as it comes to them in this particular instant. It never has anything to do with you, even when it feels like they're directly attacking, accusing or abusing you. (And from a higher perspective it is an orchestration of Life creating situations for you that allow you to clue in and become more aware of who you truly are.)

It's always the other one acting out of fear, trying to gain control, attempting to defend themselves. It has nothing to do with you.
It cannot ever.

If you are making someone else responsible for your happiness, you are giving your power away.
It's never about what happens, but what you *do* with what happens.

It's your choice.

Instead, how about being so fully connected to yourself, loving yourself unconditionally in every moment, that you don't need anyone else to show up a certain way for you?

If they choose to do so – Great!
If not – Great!

You can still choose to look at Life as being always *for* you. And even if you experience something as 'negative', know that it must be serving you in some way, or else it wouldn't have happened.

How is it making you aware of where you are out of alignment, out of integrity, with your true self, which is Love Essence?

I'm very grateful that this approach to Life was already available to me when this story happened.
(I'm diving deeper into this in my next book: *Free to Be You – Fearlessly + Unapologetically*)

So, where are YOU giving your power away?

Acknowledgments

A very warm 'Thank You' to my fellow retreat companions in this adventure: Adam Wile and his girlfriend; Francesco; Sean Bishop and Ofer Laufer; for allowing this connection, for bringing such a variety of perspectives, for co-creating this experience with me and showing up the way you did. I truly appreciate you and what you brought to our 'trip'.

Heart-felt appreciation for the shaman and his mission work at the center, introducing new ways to live in harmony with nature. To all the personnel and staff at the retreat center for their very kind and caring attention throughout.

A special 'Thank You' to my dear friend, Marci Forand, who was the first to read the draft of this story, and encouraged me to expand on the 'giving my power away' aspect and insights.

Thank you, Anna Cortez, my lovely connection and support at Lettra Press, for helping me publish this book on very short notice.

The proceeds of this book are dedicated to various environmental organizations and causes I am directly involved with (e.g. Seacology.org, the shaman's mission, solar-powered plastic recycling projects for islands and other remote areas globally).

Thank YOU for actively participating in supporting the healing of our beautiful planet Earth.

Book reviews

Shanna Jamieson takes you on a whole different trip and tells her story with humor and integrity. She takes you with her, and you can feel every experience as if you were there too. I couldn't stop reading. Her writing includes profound questions we all have about life. We can find the answers within ourselves. In this true story lack of faith lets Shanna give away her power. I saw myself doing the exact same thing.

I love this book because it is about of all us in a nutshell.

Marcela Forand, Germany

Dear Shanna,

Wow, what an educational experience! I am so relieved that your life force energy is so strong to survive.

I love how you wrote about your experiences, it's an intriguing and easy read.

Sharing this story could help a lot of people to understand what they are in for, should they be curious about Ayahuasca. You have certainly talked me out of ever trying it.

This story could help a lot of people because it's valuable lesson to not give one's power away and trust another over oneself. I have had this lesson many times myself (in other ways) and it's good to know that I am not alone in having blind faith sometimes.

There has been a fine line between trusting myself and not trusting anyone else to find a balance. I have comfort myself not being allowed to have opinions for so long, but giving my power away was such a habit out of necessity to survive that I appreciate reminders like yours. Trusting myself and the Divine higher powers is much more empowering than feeling another human should be given the power to have power over me. Your story is a good reminder of so many lessons.

Jana Kieboam, Vermont